North to Amaroqvik

by
Cheryl M. Ufkin

SCHOOL OF TOMORROW®

Lewisville, Texas

SCHOOL OF TOMORROW
P.O. Box 299000
Lewisville, Texas 75029-9000

©2000 Cheryl M. Ufkin, M.Ed.
Used by permission

Airplane on front cover: Photo courtesy of F. E. Potts
(www.fepco.com)
©1993 by F. E. Potts. All rights reserved

ISBN 1-56265-065-3
2 3 4 5 Printing/Year 04 03 02
Printed in the United States of America

DEDICATED TO:

Christian youth everywhere. May you know the joy and excitement of serving Jesus on a daily basis.

My daughter-in-law, who, through her avid reading, inspired me to write for youth.

My son, who persuaded me to write a boys' series.

Dr. William J. Wilson, my English professor, who awakened a passion within me for writing.

And of course God, by Whom we live, breathe, and have our very being.

SPECIAL RECOGNITION:

To my husband, for urging me to share this book with School of Tomorrow®.

And to Mrs. Jackie Burk, who took the pictures out of my mind and put them on paper.

TABLE OF CONTENTS

PREFACE

North to Amaroqvik (ăm·ə·rōk′vĭk) is a novel set in the Canadian Northwest. Though the story is based on many experiences of the author and her family, the characters and setting are fictional.

Amaroqvik, which means "place of the wolf," is named after a settlement that once existed but is now uninhabited and serves as a traditional hunting ground. Although the village of Amaroqvik is a fictional settlement, it is similar to many other villages, towns, and hamlets in the Northwest Territories of Canada.

Amaroqvik is located in the delta of the Mackenzie River. This region is the homeland of the Inuit (ĭn′ōō·ĭt) people. The Inuit were formerly called Eskimos. The Inuit who live near the Mackenzie River are called Inuvialuits (ĭ·nōō′vē·à′lōō·ĭts).

The Mackenzie River is very important to the people living in this region because it provides them with both food and transportation. The spring breakup of ice on the river is still celebrated in various festivals.

Animals are necessary for the survival of these northern people. Arctic animals are used for food, and their hides provide clothing and shelter. Traditional hunting lodges are constructed of sod and timber and then are covered with caribou skins.

Many arctic animals, including wolves, rabbits, and ptarmigan (tär′mə•gən) change color with the seasons. The ptarmigan is a bird whose feathers are brown, black, and tan in the summer to blend with the ground where it nests. In the winter, the ptarmigan's white feathers blend with the snow.

Because animals play such an important part in their lives, Inuit people are often given animal names. Along with their animal names, they generally are given an English or Inuvialuit first and last name too.

Now let's journey north to the land of ice and snow and the midnight sun.

Chapter 1
NORTH TO AMAROQVIK

As Andy Johnson looked out the cockpit window, he could see ice forming on the wings. "Not again," he thought. The danger of crashing was so great in these small, single-engine planes when ice built up on the wings. Any number of things could go wrong, but the most imminent was the freezing-up of the ailerons. If they froze tight, he would lose control.

Should he go on and risk the danger, or should he land at Lake Okanagan? If he landed within the next forty-five minutes or so, he would be safe, but what of the Milligans? Their baby was running a high fever, so they desperately needed the antibiotics he was carrying. And the entire settlement was waiting for his shipment of cornmeal to arrive. What a dilemma! Again he considered whether he should continue north over the treacherous Rocky Mountains to Amaroqvik or play it safe by landing in the Okanagan Valley.

Andy had deliberated only a few prayerful moments when he remembered how God had called him five years earlier to aid missionaries in remote areas as a missionary pilot. His decision was made. No matter what the cost, he must go on.

CHAPTER 2
ROYAL CANADIAN AIR FORCE

Beyond the clear blue sky that stretched before him, Andy could see a mist forming over the mountaintops. And through the mist, some 2,400 kilometers (1,500 miles) to the north, lay the village of Amaroqvik. Amaroqvik was not a pleasant town. In the summer, mud was everywhere, and it seemed the world's largest mosquitoes infested the place. These mosquitoes were the size of wasps, and when they bit you, you knew it. They were so bad that the residents nicknamed them the Royal Canadian Air Force—if their village were ever attacked, the enemy would retreat as soon as the mosquitoes came out. As bad as the mosquitoes were, though, the worst part of summer in Amaroqvik was the unrelenting light. Because the village lay so far north, the sun never completely set for two months. In July, midnight was just a sort of dusk.

Winter was even worse because it lasted so long. From September through May, the region was a frozen wasteland with no access in or out except by air, dogsled, or snowmobile. In the dead of winter, November through January, darkness prevailed—high noon still had a deep dusk about it. The continual darkness brought a sort of gloom to the place that was hard to live with through the winter months. Only Jesus, the Light within, could give cheer during those dreary months.

Despite the discomforts, a majestic beauty did exist in this frozen land to which God had called Patrick Milligan and his family to minister. The people living in this region had never heard the Gospel, and government workers who had been sent to Amaroqvik needed a place to worship. So here the Milligans were, locked off from the rest of the world, surrounded by mountains to the west, a vast wilderness to the south and east, and the tempestuous sea to the north.

CHAPTER 3
SNOWBIRD'S FLIGHT PATH

"Dear God, please be with me," Andy whispered as he soared over the towering pines. He knew getting to Amaroqvik meant seven grueling hours of bumpy flight. For about the next four hours, he would be flying over mountains and pines. After that would be three hours with taiga and then tundra below him before he arrived in Amaroqvik. Once there, the airstrip was certainly nothing to get excited about. It was just a smoothed-out stretch of ice with lights shining on it. At least there were lights; it could be worse.

"Snowbird to base," Andy called over the radio.

The tower in Kelowna responded, "Come in, Snowbird."

"I am reporting my flight path to Amaroqvik."

"In this weather, Snowbird? The wind is west at 64 kilometers (40 miles) per hour and picking up."

"I am aware of that, but I'm carrying medicine and food."

"The temperature is currently 23 degrees below 0 Celsius (-10°F) at ground level, but at your altitude it is nearly 34 degrees below (-30°F). Be advised, we do **not** recommend that you continue on this flight path."

"I must continue," Andy stated firmly. "Now, please chart my course so you can track me if need be."

11

"Go ahead, Snowbird, but you are taking your life into your own hands."

"God's hands, to be more precise," Andy said to himself.

As he signed off, the controller muttered, "So we can track him if need be? 'Need be,' he says! In this weather it is inevitable. The man is crazy."

The noise of the droning engine filled the cockpit once again. Now it was just Andy, the icy blue sky, and God. Andy thought, "Just think how lonely it would be up here if I did not have the Lord with me."

This stretch of the trip was truly the most beautiful. The forested mountainsides with snow-capped peaks were certainly magnificent. Then, abruptly, near the top of each peak, the trees stopped. This marked change in vegetation was called the tree line. The air was so cold above the tree line that even the hardiest trees could not survive.

Every now and then, the mountains exercised their fearful power. Rockslides and avalanches were common. Below him, Andy could see where the village of Owapunik had once been. Nearly four years before, when he was flying in these parts, a huge rockslide had ripped down the mountain, completely burying the village. Today all that was left as a grim reminder of that tragic event was a mound of granite boulders. Since the soil was completely buried under huge rocks, nothing could grow at that spot. The mound of stones glared from the side of the mountain like a giant tombstone for the whole village.

Andy always got a sad feeling when he passed that spot—so full of memories he was. But the past was the past. He must go on, and right now he had to get to Amaroqvik.

Checking his gauges, he could see that everything was stable, but ice was continuing to build on the outside of the plane. The small aircraft was already at its maximum weight due to the load of cornmeal, dried fish, medicines, and other supplies he was carrying in addition to his heavy fuel load. He certainly did not need the added weight of the ice buildup.

In spite of these conditions, Andy felt at peace. A voice in his head seemed to say, "Be still, and know that I am God."

CHAPTER 4
TRUST

Icy winds were howling outside the Milligans' small, four-room, wood-framed home in the village of Amaroqvik. Mrs. Milligan knew she should not complain. Her little house, drafty as it was, seemed nearly a mansion in comparison to the dwellings made of sod and animal skins in which some of the residents lived. The government workers here on oil-drilling assignments had it no better. The aluminum mobile units, which served as their temporary homes, seemed to attract the cold. Huddled near the oil stove, she sat in her rocking chair and remembered the lovely farm home she had left in Oregon. She was dreaming of the pink apple blossoms in spring when baby Jonathan's cry jerked her back to reality. She clutched him close to her body, trying to comfort him. Poor child; he had had a fever of 40 degrees Celsius (104°F) for nearly three days now, and nothing she did relieved it.

"Patrick," she whispered to her husband, "what can we do? Jonathan is burning up." Her eyes filled with tears as she spoke. That helpless feeling which a mother has when her child's welfare is beyond her control welled up inside her.

"Sweetheart," he replied, "trust. Just trust. That is the best thing we can do. The sponge baths and aspirin have not worked, and we have no other medicine. We have prayed incessantly these last three days. Jonathan is in God's hands, so we need to simply trust God and know that whatever happens is in God's total plan for our lives."

Pastor Milligan was so peaceful and calm. No matter what happened, his faith never wavered. One time last spring, a hungry bear wandered into the village. He knocked over garbage cans and scavenged whatever he could find. The Milligans' daughter, Alisha, was out in the yard digging a spot to plant some potatoes. She had not spotted the bear yet. Her mother, who was washing dishes and looking out the window, saw the bear and let out a bloodcurdling scream. At that, the poor, frightened bear turned and ran. He was headed straight for the garden patch where Alisha stood frozen with fear. Just then her father opened the door, stretched out his hand, and in a firm voice prayed, "In the name of Jesus, bear, I command you to stop!" The confused bear stopped, turned to the left, and lumbered off into the woods.

Just as God communicated with the animals in Noah's day and shut the lions' mouths for Daniel, God did the same for the Milligans that cool May morning.

Pastor Milligan stood on God's Word. God is the same yesterday, today, and forever.

CHAPTER 5
THE LAST SUPPER

Sea Gull, a dear member of the church in Amaroqvik, was fixing her family's evening meal of fried seal and cornmeal mush. She turned to her husband, White Bear, and said, "I know we have only this last bit of cornmeal in the barrel, but I feel I should take supper to the Milligans tonight. Mrs. Milligan must be exhausted. I know she has been up nearly around the clock these last three days caring for little Jonathan. You know they have always helped us, no matter what."

White Bear, who had been a Believer for only a few months, could not quite understand giving away their last meal. "But, Sea Gull, we have five children of our own to feed, and if you make a double batch of mush tonight, we will have none left for tomorrow. Who knows when the supply plane will arrive in this weather."

"Dear Husband, you know I would never dispute you, but please allow me to tell you about a lady in the Bible. She was a poor widow lady with a son to support and had only one handful of meal and a bit of oil left when God's prophet Elijah came along.

"The prophet told the lady, 'Please bring me some water and a piece of bread.'

"The lady said, 'I would, sir, but I have only enough to make one last meal; then my son and I will lie down and die, for we have no more food.'

"The prophet told her not to fear but to make some bread for him first; then she could make some for her son and herself. Elijah promised that God would supply. She obeyed the prophet; and, you know, dear, her barrel of meal never went empty and neither did her jar of oil! God took care of her and her son because she took care of God's prophet. Pastor Milligan is the man God sent to us, and I feel we should help him and his family."

"Well," White Bear said slowly, "if you really believe God will not allow our children to go hungry, go ahead and make supper for the Milligans. I still have much to learn about this God of Heaven. You have been going to the mission church for three years now; so you have heard much from the Holy Book, but I have heard only a little. I only wish I could read so I could learn more about God. All I know from the Bible is what I hear from you and what I hear at the mission from Pastor Milligan. I am so grateful they started a school for the village children. Our little ones will be able to read the Bible for themselves. Do you suppose an old man like me could learn to read?"

"Of course, dear. Just speak to Mrs. Milligan. I am sure she could teach you just like she does the

children." Then Sea Gull set about to prepare enough
seal and mush for two families.

CHAPTER 6
THE SCRABBLE GAME

Alisha and her brother Patrick Jr. were at Sea Gull's house playing Scrabble with her three oldest children. Mrs. Milligan had allowed them to go over there to play for the afternoon so that little Jonathan could sleep.

Sea Gull's house was extremely small, with only two rooms. One room was used for sitting, eating, cooking, and general daily living. The other room was used for sleeping. The bathroom was a little wooden building behind their house. Sea Gull's house, like that of most of the residents, did not have running water. In the winter months, she simply stepped outside and scooped up some fresh snow to melt. This water was used for cooking, bathing, drinking, or whatever else was needed. In the summer, she generally sent one of the children to the stream with a bucket to get water.

Even though the Milligans and a few others had running water in their houses, it did not mean much in the winter months. For days at a time, the pipes were frozen and no water could come into the house.

"Alisha, what word could I make with the letters XWZBLOL?" asked Little Bear. Little Bear was only six years old, so he did not know many words.

"Well," Alisha replied, "you could make *box* or *lox.*"

"What's lox?"

"That is the pink, salty salmon meat we eat in the spring."

"Oh, I remember. Okay. I'll put *lox* for my word. Your turn, Snow Goose."

Little Bear's older sister, Snow Goose, and Alisha were best friends, and they were nearly the same age. Alisha was twelve and Snow Goose was eleven, so they knew many words.

"Well, here goes," said Snow Goose. "I'm going to put the word *oboe.*"

"You took my place," complained Little Ptarmigan, her eight-year-old sister. "I was going to build off the letter *O.*"

"I'm sorry. I didn't know you were going to play there. Maybe I can help you find another spot for a word."

"No! I quit. You always get all the good spots."

"Come on," encouraged Alisha, "we'll help you."

"No fair. You guys are smarter than I am. You know more words. I'm just dumb, and I don't **want** your help!"

"Little Ptarmigan, that's not true," answered Snow Goose gently. "We've just been in school longer, that is all. When you get older, you will know more words too. Please play with us."

"Okay," Little Ptarmigan replied hesitantly, "but I don't know where to play."

"I see a place!" called Patrick Jr. "You could build up from Little Bear's *X*. Let that be your last letter. What letters do you have?"

"Children, dinner time. Patrick Jr., Alisha, please take this seal and mush home with you so your mother will not have to cook tonight. Tell her that White Bear and I are praying for little Jonathan. We will see you at church tonight."

"Good-bye, Sea Gull, and thank you for supper. I know Mom will appreciate it."

"Bye, guys. See you later," Patrick Jr. called.

The two children set out through the howling wind and the swirling snow to their house.

"I'm glad we don't live far," Alisha said to her brother. "I'm freezing!"

CHAPTER 7
WIND SHEAR

Darkness enveloped the little plane. Looking at his charts and gauges, Andy could tell he was near Norman Wells.

"Only about two more hours to go," he thought. "I should be able to make it."

Suddenly, the small plane jerked and started to lose altitude. Down, down, down it plunged. Andy's heart pumped wildly. Just about 100 meters (330 feet) below him, he could see the tops of the trees. Only moments earlier, they had been completely invisible because he was so high in the clouds.

"Snowbird to control tower!"

"We read you, Snowbird. This is Norman Wells. Go ahead."

"I hit a wind shear and dropped 1,200 meters (3,900 feet). I'm cruising just above the treetops."

"What's your altimeter reading?"

"Two hundred meters (660 feet)."

"Pull up. You are flying dangerously low."

"I'm pulling. I'm pulling, but nothing is happening."

"You must keep trying. One more wind shear at your altitude and you'll crash."

CHAPTER 8
TRUST NOT IN CHARIOTS

Little Jonathan's fever was rising. It was 40.3 degrees Celsius (104.5°F) now. Of course, Mrs. Milligan's fear was that he would have convulsions, but she knew she must have faith. At just that time Alisha and Patrick Jr. burst through the door.

"Hi, Mom!" the two called simultaneously. "Guess what?"

"Sea Gull fixed us dinner—seal and mush," Alisha reported.

"And it sure smells good!" Patrick Jr. added.

"What a blessing that lady is. I know she can't have any more food than we do, but here she is thinking of others instead of herself. She certainly is an example of someone with Godly character."

"Yes, Mom, you're right," Alisha responded. "If I had realized she might be running low, I would not have accepted it."

"That's okay, dear. It was meant to be."

After a nearly silent dinner, the children got dressed for the Wednesday night church service. Mrs. Milligan had been praying for Jonathan all day. Now it brought her great comfort to know that all the people who gathered at church tonight would also be praying for him. The thought of God's people praying together gave her renewed assurance of God's presence and of His watchful care over Jonathan.

"Okay, children, are you ready to go?" Mrs. Milligan called out. "Patrick Jr., you'll have to drive the snowmobile, and you two must sit close together to keep warm."

Pastor Milligan had left an hour earlier to pray and get the church building warmed up. A kerosene stove in the middle of the one-room church building was the only source of heat, and, since he wanted God's people to be comfortable, he always lit it well ahead of time. That particular night, Pastor Milligan tearfully pled with God for the healing of his younger son and for the arrival of the medicine. But he concluded his prayer as he always did with, "Your will be done."

A few at a time, the faithful members of the Amaroqvik mission church began to trickle in, with snow falling off their boots and parkas. It felt toasty warm in the small building after such a blustery trek to get there. The snow quickly melted into little puddles all across the plank floor and seeped into cracks between the planks, which swelled shut in the warm summer months. Everything shrank during the freezing arctic winters but returned to normal during the summer.

"We'll begin our service tonight with hymn number 132," Pastor Milligan announced, "'The Old Rugged Cross.'"

The members of the small congregation joyfully sang out the words as they remembered their own recent salvation. Pastor Milligan's text that evening was Ephesians 6:1–3: "Children, obey your parents in the Lord: for this is right. Honour thy father and mother; which is the first commandment with promise; That it may be well with thee, and thou mayest live long on the earth."

As part of the service, the church family shared prayer requests. The two most urgent needs were for the arrival of the mission plane and, of course, for little Jonathan.

Pastor Milligan and the entire congregation earnestly prayed: "Dear Father God, we give You little Jonathan. We humbly beg You to heal him of this illness for Your glory. Just as You told the children of Israel not to trust in the chariots of Egypt but to trust in You, we are looking to You and trusting You to heal this child. We also ask for Your protection for Andy as he travels here with the needed supplies. We pray in the Lord Jesus' name. Amen."

Joy and peace settled over the entire congregation. They felt an assurance that their prayers had been heard and were being answered. They were being answered, but not necessarily in the way they expected. Little did they know that, some 400 kilometers (250 miles) away, Andy was lying in a snowdrift, dazed—his plane demolished in the trees.

CHAPTER 9

SUPPLY PLANE MISSING

"Good morning, dear," Pastor Milligan chortled to his wife as she was stretching and waking up.

She hadn't fallen asleep until nearly 3 a.m., so she wasn't quite as chipper as her husband.

He fairly glowed as he continued, "Honey, guess what? Jonathan's fever broke early this morning! I got up right after you went to bed and sat and rocked him. I kept holding him close and praying, and at 4:20 he began sweating. The fever had broken! Isn't God wonderful?"

"Yes, dear, God is wonderful. This just proves that God is greater than any medicine. It's a new morning and we have a healthy baby Jonathan. Let's thank God together."

They knelt and prayed and rejoiced by the side of their bed. Hearing all the happy commotion, Patrick Jr. and Alisha ran into the bedroom.

"Dad, Mom, what's up?" queried Patrick Jr.

"The Lord has healed your little brother," Pastor Milligan proclaimed.

"Oh, I knew He would. I just didn't know when," Patrick Jr. responded.

Alisha was too overcome with emotion to speak. She just ran over to the crib, picked up baby Jonathan, and clutched him to her chest, tears streaming down her face.

An hour later at the breakfast table, the subject turned from the bliss of Jonathan's recovery to the whereabouts of Andy and his supply plane. After a big bowl of hot cornmeal mush with butter and sugar on it, Alisha excused herself from the table to get ready for school. Patrick Jr. was right at her heels.

Mrs. Milligan spoke to her husband, "You know, dear, I am very grateful that Jonathan is well and we don't need the medicine, but this mush is the last breakfast food we have in the house. We don't have much of anything else either. While I'm at school today, would you call the control tower at Norman Wells and ask if they know where Andy is? Perhaps he spent the night there because of the weather."

"Certainly, dear. I think that's a good idea. Now, you and the children get ready for school while I run over to get the fire started. I'll come right back and keep Jonathan with me today so he can get plenty of rest."

The church building also served as the school, clinic, library, local meeting hall, and virtually anything else that was needed. The desks were pushed neatly against the walls whenever the building was being used for purposes other than school. Five mornings a week, the room fairly bustled with activity as the desks and chairs were put back in place for school.

Jonathan usually went to school with Mrs. Milligan and played in his playpen while she helped the older children with their studies. On occasion, Sea Gull watched him at her house, but most days Sea Gull came over to the school, at least during reading hour. She claimed it was to help Mrs. Milligan, but secretly the Milligans knew it was her way of learning to read better herself. Sea Gull dearly loved hearing the Bible stories, and, like most of the older village people, she had had very little opportunity for an education. By daily listening to the children read aloud and following along in her book, Sea Gull had learned a lot.

When Pastor Milligan came in the front door, shaking the snow off himself, Mrs. Milligan called, "Well, children, it's 8 o'clock. Time to go to school."

Although Pastor Milligan was quite concerned about Andy's whereabouts, he did not show it. After Mrs. Milligan and the two older children left for school, he found the phone number and called the control tower at Norman Wells.

"Hello, this is Pastor Milligan in Amaroqvik. We were expecting our supply plane to arrive last night. Andy Johnson is always on schedule, and since he did

31

not show up last night, we are quite concerned. Did he radio in to you or spend the night there?"

"He did radio here, but he did not land, at least not on this airstrip. He said he had hit a wind shear and had lost altitude. His last message was so fuzzy we couldn't make it out, and we have had no further word. If he didn't make it to your place, I fear the worst. He may be down, sir."

CHAPTER 10
SEARCH PARTY

Pastor Milligan immediately notified his wife to dismiss school for the day. As soon as Mrs. Milligan and the children arrived home to care for Jonathan, Pastor Milligan went about town to relay the information about Andy. White Bear suggested they form two teams and begin a thorough search between Amaroqvik and Great Bear Lake. That was a vast stretch of wilderness some 500 kilometers (310 miles) long and seemingly endless kilometers (miles) wide, depending how far off course Andy had veered when he hit the wind shear.

The men agreed with White Bear's suggestion, and he headed up the search effort. They gathered all the able-bodied men who owned either a snowmobile or a dog team and sled. That included nearly everyone, since those were the two major modes of transportation during the long winter months. The permanent residents were all like family members who helped one another in time of need, so everyone was willing to use his supplies to assist in the search for Andy.

"Pastor Milligan, may I make a suggestion?" asked White Bear.

"Of course. What is it?"

"Let's set off in opposite directions. I'll head southeast in a diagonal line toward the northern edge of Great Bear Lake. You head almost due south and follow the bank of the Mackenzie River and then cut over toward the western edge of the lake. That trail is easier to travel because you go alongside the river. No disrespect, Pastor, but I know this country better than you do."

"Thank you very much, White Bear. I appreciate your concern, and I think your suggestion is wise."

"May I make one more suggestion?"

"What is it?"

"I believe, in the dead of winter like this, we should not be out any more than ten days. We all have families to care for, you know. We must not die of exposure."

Pastor Milligan respected the wisdom of White Bear when it came to dealing with his harsh homeland. "You are correct," replied Pastor Milligan. "Even though we are concerned for Andy's welfare, we must take precautions. What do you say we each travel five days in our respective directions, search around for a day, then turn around and come back to Amaroqvik?"

"I think that sounds like a reasonable plan," agreed White Bear.

The wives gathered dried fish, and the few who had cornmeal left made fried corn cakes for the men to take on their journey. Of course, the men packed hunting supplies and hoped to encounter some "food" while they were out. Soon the sleds and snowmobiles were laden with blankets, fire starter, matches, small tents, and sundry other items.

Nearly the entire village gathered at the church-school-town meeting hall building. With the supplies loaded, all present gathered for prayer—not only for Andy but also for their own safety.

Many pitfalls awaited anyone on the trail. Sometimes the snow drifted to look like level ground when in reality it hid a gully. A heavy vehicle could break the frozen top crust and sink 2 to 3 meters (6 to 10 feet). Snow would then fall in and ruin the supplies. Even more dreaded was ice that formed a shell over a rushing stream but broke under any weight. The icy waters would chill a person so thoroughly that, if he didn't drown, he would almost surely die of hypothermia or pneumonia. That's where teamwork came in. The searchers spaced themselves so that if one landed in a pitfall, the others would not lose sight of him. That was difficult to accomplish, though, because sometimes the snow was falling so thickly that you could barely see 2 meters (6 feet) ahead of you. Caution was definitely needed on the journey.

"Good-bye, and God bless you, Pastor," White Bear called as he waved a mittened hand.

"And the Lord guide, direct, and keep you, Brother!" Pastor Milligan shouted back over the roar of twenty-one snowmobile engines and six teams of yipping dogs.

The women, children, and village elders all reluctantly waved good-bye as the two parties departed. A heaviness settled over the village because everyone was aware of the dangers of the trail.

CHAPTER 11
CRUMPLED STEEL

Andy squeezed his body through the narrow opening beneath the wing where his aircraft had cracked open during the sudden impact after falling from the sky and crashing into the treetops. "Thank You, Lord, for the treetops! If my plane had hit with full impact, it would have burst into flames and killed me instantly."

The treetops had acted as a buffer, slowing the plane to the extent that it had landed as a crumpled, but still largely intact, pile of wreckage.

The propeller had been ripped off and had flown through the trees, landing several hundred meters (yards) away from the wreckage. The starboard ski was totally bent, as the weight of the tilted plane rested on that side. On the left side, the ski was still intact and the wing stood up in the air. All the supplies, which had shifted during Andy's tumble from the sky, made it difficult to move around inside the plane.

The doors were frozen shut, which was a common occurrence at these temperatures. Normally that did not pose a problem, as Andy would use his body weight to crack open the ice seal by pushing his left shoulder into the door. Now, however, with the small aircraft sitting at such an angle, he could not get the leverage he needed

to push the door open. On the starboard side, all the supplies were piled on top of the door. The easiest solution was to wriggle his way out through the crack where the left wing had been partially ripped from the fuselage of the plane.

He wormed his way out, feet first. He clung to the edge with his frozen fingertips, looking at the 4-meter (13-foot) drop beneath him for a few seconds before letting go.

"Thank You, Lord, for sparing me," whispered Andy as he landed in the soft snow.

"Well, I made it, and I'm alive," said Andy, half to himself and half to God. "Good thing I was wearing my seat belt, or I would have been beaten to pieces. The ride down through those trees was wilder than the Dizzy Drop ride at the Polk County Fair last year. Whoa! The ground is spinning." Andy tried to clamber to his feet but fell dizzily back into the soft snow. He lay there a few minutes, too dizzy to move. His head was pounding.

Coming fully alert, Andy sat up. "I suppose I should just sit here a moment and collect my thoughts. My first priority is to keep warm." Andy reached into the pockets of the red snowmobile suit he was wearing and pulled out his down-filled, black nylon mittens.

"If I can just make it to the Mackenzie River, I should find a trapper's cabin."

Though trapping was not nearly as popular as it had once been, there were still people who did it for a living. Trappers usually left a few supplies in their cabins for passersby who might need them or for themselves on their return.

"Okay, I think I can stand up now."

Andy struggled to his feet and slipped into the heavy backpack lying beside him. All the supplies he had managed to salvage from the wreck were in his backpack. The cornmeal and flour had been ruined in the crash when the plastic kerosene jugs had split and leaked their contents onto everything. The only salvageable items were six tins of milk that Mrs. Milligan had ordered for Jonathan, five tins of sardines in mustard sauce that were Pastor Milligan's personal favorite, a metal canister of wooden matches, and one miraculously unbroken jar out of a case of pickled beets. Andy had also filled his empty coffee thermos with kerosene from one of the leaking containers, thinking he might need it later for fire starter. The only other item Andy had tossed out of the plane was his leather overnight pouch containing one pair of clean underwear, two pairs of wool socks, toothpaste, toothbrush, shaving cream, razor, after-shave lotion, and the compass he had ripped off the instrument panel.

"Well, even though this pack weighs a ton, it isn't much to live on for very long," mused Andy.

"At least I have my hunting knife. That thing has been with me for five years now, through the swamp, the rain forest, and now the frozen North."

Andy kept the long hunting knife in a sheath strapped to his right leg whenever he flew. He had survived many strange mishaps during his last five years as a missionary pilot throughout the Western Hemisphere.

"By God's grace, I've always made it before, so I'll make it this time too. I am just not sure how."

Andy's rugged good looks were still intact despite his fall. No bones were broken, but his right cheekbone was bruised where his face had bounced against the instrument panel, and his right elbow and knee ached where they had slammed into the control stick when the plane finally jerked to a stop at a forty-five degree angle. He stood there among the trees in his red snowmobile suit, his muscular 2-meter (6-foot) frame silhouetted against the snow, a few blond locks of curly hair sticking out from under his black wool stocking cap. Though he was big and strong, he looked so small and vulnerable standing there alone in the vast wilderness.

"Good-bye, Bethany," he called. (That was what he had named his small aircraft.) "You've been a good friend to many people, but I'm afraid you're never going to fly again. You look in pretty rough shape. I'll come back to visit you in the spring and see if there is anything I can do for you."

He set his face westward and began to walk away from the only familiar thing in sight.

Chapter 12
CARIBOU STAMPEDE

"Alisha," called Mrs. Milligan late that afternoon, "I sent the last of the food we had in the house with your father this morning. Of course, if he had known that, he would have forbidden me to do so, but I just thought of something. Do you remember where you planted potatoes last year? Perhaps a few of them eluded you when you dug them up. I know it will be difficult in this frozen ground, but why don't you and Patrick Jr. go out and dig. I believe that, if Patrick stands on the spade while you rock it back and forth, you can penetrate the soil."

"All right, Mom," called Alisha as she bounded out of the room to get her parka. "It sounds like a treasure hunt. We'll be searching for buried treasure, and the treasure will be potatoes!"

By now, White Bear's search party was well away from the village. He had not planned on doing any hunting for the first day or two, as the village women had pooled their resources and laden them with about two days' worth of food. But suddenly a herd of caribou dashed crazily across their path. Startled by the noise of the oncoming snowmobiles, the caribou dispersed, running wildly in all directions.

"Stop your engines!" yelled White Bear at the top of his lungs, but to no avail. The pounding of hoofs and the roar of the engines were so loud that nobody heard him. He stopped his vehicle and crouched low. As the other snowmobiles forged ahead, the scattered caribou became even more frightened. About 27 meters (30 yards) ahead of him, he could see a caribou clumsily hurdle his cousin Brown Bear's snowmobile. In that split second, White Bear called out a prayer, "Oh, God of Pastor Milligan, God Who made the stars, protect my cousin."

The sharp, cup-shaped hoofs of the caribou just missed Brown Bear's head as the bulky animal leaped over him and galloped away through the taiga.

At that moment, out of nowhere, a huge caribou came running directly toward the snowmobile where White Bear was crouched almost level with the handlebars. It arched over him in a single bound. He reached over to the holder he had mounted for his 30-06 rifle and pulled it out. He grasped the trigger and fired at the fleeing caribou. The animal slowed momentarily, then took off. White Bear aimed a little more to the right, then fired again. The animal fell over on its side with a great thud. It was a well-aimed shot, and the heavy creature died instantly.

Hearing the shots, the rest of the party stopped, as the remaining caribou took cover in the woods on the other side of the clearing. All the men were breathing heavily, hearts pounding, as they convened.

"What happened? Are you all right?" asked Brown Bear as he approached his cousin.

"I'm fine; how about you?" asked White Bear. "I saw that caribou's hind hoofs just miss your head. I said a little prayer for you to the God of the mission church."

"I'm glad you did," replied Brown Bear. "I thought I was going to be a dead man."

"Me too," sighed White Bear.

"Well, looks like we will have plenty of meat now," called out Major Burgess as he pulled up on his snowmobile. He was a retired military man working in the oil fields around Amaroqvik. He had joined the search party more for the adventure than out of a self-sacrificing love for mankind.

"You're right about that," replied White Bear, glancing at the downed animal. "He must weigh 320 kilograms (700 pounds). Let's dress him and hit the trail for another hour before setting up camp for the night."

Meanwhile, back in Amaroqvik, God was also supplying sustenance.

"Alisha, look, look!" called Patrick Jr. excitedly as his spade hit an entire mound of potatoes. "You put them in the bag while I work them loose with the fork."

"Okay," Alisha gleefully replied. "Mom will be thrilled."

That mound yielded about 2 kilograms (5 pounds) of potatoes, and they found a few other stragglers that had been missed during fall harvest.

"Let's go in now," called Alisha. "I'm freezing to death, and this is more than enough potatoes for supper."

Once in the warm house, the frozen potatoes thawed into a soggy mess.

"Alisha," Mrs. Milligan called, "please put on a pot of snow to boil. I'll have to cook these potatoes right now, or they'll spoil."

She quickly peeled and placed the grayish-colored potatoes into the pot of melted snow.

"They may look a little off-color due to freezing, but they'll taste fine," assured Mrs. Milligan as she added some salt and dried parsley leaves.

The two treasure hunters stood over the pot, sniffing the delightful aroma of the fruit of their labors.

"Mom, may we please take some of these potatoes over to Sea Gull when they are cooked?" queried Alisha.

"Oh, of course! Take her half of them. We must have over 2 kilograms (5 pounds) here. And it's a good thing too, since Andy's plane hasn't arrived."

CHAPTER 13
A PICKLED-BEET POPSICLE

"I was so certain I would find a cabin on this river," muttered Andy. "I've walked for two days. Now I'm beginning the third, and I have not even seen the remains of an old cabin. At least I found the river. I won't ever really be 'lost' as long as I follow it. I still have some canned milk and sardines. By the time they run out, surely I will have found a cabin with some supplies left in it."

Andy trudged along in silence. The deep snow made it difficult to walk. He was so cold his feet ached, and his face felt numb even though he had taken the wool socks out of his satchel and tied them around his face. He felt **so** alone. He had not seen a creature for two days except for one small flock of ptarmigan. The silence and vastness of the area, with nothing new in sight, coupled with the throbbing pain in his right cheekbone were beginning to wear down Andy's spirits.

"I must get a hold of myself. I **cannot** let myself get depressed. If I get low in spirit, I'll die. My mind **must** remain strong, no matter how hopeless the circumstances look.

"God, **please** help me. Please let me feel Your presence right now. I feel so alone. This country is so big, so empty. I need You now, God. Please help me."

On the day of the crash, Andy had made it to the river by nightfall and had spent the night burrowed under a pile of fallen trees. To conserve supplies, he drank only one can of milk, reasoning that he had eaten a good meal that morning in Kelowna. On day two, he drank one can of milk and ate one can of sardines in mustard sauce, but it simply was not enough food to give him the energy his body was demanding to keep him warm and to trudge through the deep snow.

Andy left the river's edge and went into the trees to sit on a fallen log. "I guess I'd better eat lunch since I haven't had anything to eat yet today. It's exhausting wading through this soft snow, but, if it were cold enough to form an ice crust, I'd freeze to death. I guess I'd better be grateful for soft snow. Now, let's see. What shall I eat for lunch today? Sardines and milk or milk and sardines? H-m-m."

After eating the sardines, Andy rummaged through his pack and discovered the pickled beets. The beets had now frozen and expanded to the point that the jar had shattered into several large pieces. Andy "peeled off" the glass from the solid lump of pickled beets suspended in frozen brine. He carefully wiped the surface of the beet ice cube with his bare fingertips to check for any remaining shards of glass. Finding none, he proceeded to gnaw around the edges as if it were a Popsicle.

"Um-m, this is tasty—frozen pickled-beet juice. I just can't wait to get back to civilization and share this recipe."

The sardines in mustard sauce were already taking effect on Andy's system by the time he started eating his "beet Popsicle." His strength was coming back, and he was a little more cheerful.

"Well, I guess it's time to set out again. Soon it will be too dark to keep walking, and it sure would be a blessing to find a cabin to sleep in tonight."

CHAPTER 14
PLENTY TO EAT

On the evening of the sixth day of the search, Pastor Milligan's team returned to Amaroqvik. Cold and exhausted, the men were grateful to get to their warm cabins. They had searched for three days in the more open country and had not even made it to the more heavily forested area when a blinding snowstorm forced them to retreat. Had they forged ahead in such conditions, they certainly would have died.

"I feel terrible that we abandoned the search, Minerva." (Minerva was Mrs. Milligan's first name, but he rarely called her that. In front of the children and the congregation she was "Mrs. Milligan.") "I feel so guilty, so worthless. Andy is out there somewhere alone, and we just gave up," Pastor Milligan chided himself.

"You've done all you could," comforted his wife. "You are not in control of the elements. You did the right thing. You were the leader of your team, and you decided that, rather than jeopardize the lives of all the men on your team, it would be prudent to return."

"I guess you're right, dear. I just wish we could have made it at least to the more forested area. In the open country, we could see for kilometers (miles) and we saw nothing, but maybe if we had reached the forested area, we could have seen some signs of a crash."

"You can't go on chiding yourself. You made a decision, and it was a wise one. If Andy did crash, he probably didn't live through it. You know those single-engine planes have a tendency to burn on impact."

"I don't even want to consider that, Minerva. Surely Andy must be out there somewhere. Maybe he did land on Great Bear Lake. He has skis, so he could have just put down on the ice and been fine. Of course, it is 600 kilometers (370 miles) to Great Bear Lake, and Andy may not have even made it that far. With the blizzard conditions we're having, nobody can even get there to search until spring. I just feel so helpless."

"I know exactly how you feel, Patrick. That's how I felt when baby Jonathan was so sick. And remember what you told me? Trust. Just trust and believe. If Andy is still alive, then God will take care of him. Remember the Scripture that not even one sparrow falls to the ground without God taking notice of it. So how much more will He take care of Andy? God's Word never fails. We must trust."

Just then the roar of snowmobile engines and the yipping dogs of two sled teams broke the silence of winter. It was White Bear's search party pulling into Amaroqvik. They, too, had encountered the blizzard as it blew its way eastward across the tundra and the taiga. They were also forced to turn around and head back.

Pulling up in front of the town hall-church-school building, the men called out, "Fresh caribou, fresh caribou!"

Those words sent the whole village rushing out to meet the men. Dressed into neat, long slabs, there was enough meat for every family in the village to take home a huge chunk. What rejoicing! After a week of scarcity, there was abundance. The whole town was thrilled.

Mrs. Milligan decided to grind a piece of their meat. "Tacos tonight!" she announced.

That evening the entire Milligan family sat around the table, enjoying caribou tacos. "M-m-m, Mom, these taste so good!" exclaimed Patrick Jr.

"Yes, even without lettuce, tomatoes, and cheese, they're still wonderful," chimed in Alisha. "You put in just the right spices to give them a taco flavor."

"Thank you, family," replied Mrs. Milligan. "You're very kind. I had just enough flour and seal grease left to make soft tortillas. This is indeed a treat after all those potatoes last week!"

Even baby Jonathan was gumming a soft flour tortilla and grinning a toothless smile.

Pastor Milligan sat in silence, drinking in the pleasures of hearth and home. He was cozy, warm, had had a good meal, and was at peace listening to the joyful conversation of his family.

"Now, all we need are cornmeal cookies and we'd have a real feast," called out Patrick Jr.

"In the spring, son—in the spring, we'll get supplies, and I'll make you a big batch of cornmeal cookies."

CHAPTER 15
A CABIN AT LAST

Andy, weakly dragging himself, finally came to a big, round rock at the side of the river and leaned up against it.

"Oh, Lord, it's been seven days now. I just can't go on. My bones ache. I've slept under logs, in hollows, even buried in needles. I'm exhausted. I'm so hungry and weak. This is my last can of milk, and everything else is gone. Please help me, Lord."

Andy drank his can of milk and leaned back against the rock. A chinook wind had blown in and warmed the air. Peace and sleep overcame Andy, and he napped beside the rock. It was late in the afternoon when he awoke.

"I sure slept well," mused Andy, "but I wish I hadn't napped for so long. It will be fully dark soon, and I don't want to spend another night outdoors!

"I passed the mountains about an hour before I crashed," recalled Andy, "so I must be between 500 and 600 kilometers (310 and 370 miles) from Amaroqvik. Approximately another 200 kilometers (125 miles) of forest before I reach the open country. But what good will it do to reach open country? Nobody can make it this far in the winter to search for me. My best chance of survival is to stay in the shelter of the forest and keep looking for a trapper's cabin."

Andy was grateful for the clarity of thought that the nap had afforded him. He set out with renewed vigor on his search for a cabin. Stumbling over the rocks at the edge of the Mackenzie River, he kept forging ahead.

"It's too dark to go much farther. I guess I'll just go around that bend in the river and burrow out a shelter for tonight."

Just as he rounded the bend, Andy saw something shadowed against the arctic sky.

"A cabin!" he shouted. "A real cabin! Thank You, Lord!" he called out as he stumbled forward as fast as the rocks would allow.

Andy fairly burst through the door that creaked on rusty hinges. Surveying the room by the light of a match, Andy mused, "There are no usable supplies except for this tin of matches on the fireplace. The traps are all too rusty to be useful. And there's no food. From the looks of this place, it must have been empty for ten years."

A single cot was pushed up against the wall across from the fireplace. The single layer of bedsprings was rust-coated and sagging in the middle. The stuffing from the mattress was escaping in fluffy clumps through holes gnawed in the ticking, but to Andy's eyes, it might as well have been a fine bed with satin sheets.

"Yes!" he exclaimed as he flopped his body across the cot. "A real bed, not a pile of needles!" Then he began to sneeze repeatedly from the dust he had stirred up by flopping onto the mattress.

With the warm chinook wind came snow, and big, fluffy flakes drifted in through a corner window that was missing a pane. Using his trusty knife, Andy cut a piece of old, rotted tarpaulin and stuffed it into the broken window.

Sheltered from both wind and snow, Andy gazed out the window at the big, fluffy snowflakes sparkling in the moonlight as they drifted to earth. Even with no food available, he was the most contented he had been in days. Suddenly a sound arose on the wind and sent chills up his spine.

"Wolves," Andy murmured. "That's all I need. And me with only this hunting knife to protect myself."

The howling of the wolves rose on the wind, only nearer this time.

CHAPTER 16
PSALM 23

It had been a week since Andy's plane missed its anticipated arrival. Although he had not been forgotten in the hearts of the people, life went on pretty much as usual in Amaroqvik. There was plenty of caribou meat, thanks to White Bear's search party, and the villagers were in fairly good spirits, even though there wasn't much variety of other food to accompany the meat.

"Class," Mrs. Milligan announced one February morning, "we have a new student. White Bear has decided to join us, and I want you to welcome him."

After a joyous round of applause and hugs from various youngsters, White Bear settled into the routine of the school morning. He fairly glowed with anticipation, and all his earlier reservations about being too old to attend school or feeling out of place were totally dispelled by the warm welcome he received.

"Look at Psalm 23 for today's devotional reading," Mrs. Milligan continued, pointing to the brightly lettered chart paper on the wall. "We will read it together. Boys, read the first verse please; then, girls, the second verse, and we'll continue alternating. Begin, gentlemen."

"The LORD is my shepherd; I shall not want," chorused the boys, reading the purple, magic-markered words off the chart paper.

"He maketh me to lie down in green pastures: he leadeth me beside the still waters," chanted the girls as Mrs. Milligan pointed to each green-lettered word.

"He restoreth my soul: he leadeth me in the paths of righteousness for his name's sake." The boys lisped over the word *restoreth*.

The girls read the next green-lettered verse, "Yea, though I walk through the valley of the shadow of death, I will fear no evil: for thou art with me; thy rod and thy staff they comfort me."

Smoothly following into the next purple-lettered verse, the boys continued, "Thou preparest a table before me in the presence of mine enemies: thou anointest my head with oil; my cup runneth over."

"Surely goodness and mercy shall follow me all the days of my life: and I will dwell in the house of the LORD for ever," concluded the girls.

"Excellent reading, class. Everybody repeat, 'r-e-s-t-o-r-e-t-h.' Again 'r-e-s-t-o-r-e-t-h.' When you see 'th' in English words, you must put your tongue between your teeth," Mrs. Milligan instructed. "Now one more time, and let me see those tongues, 'r-e-s-t-o-r-e-t-h.'"

There was no "th" sound in their home language, so the children had a very difficult time pronouncing words with "th" in them.

"Now, I'm going to divide you into six groups, and each group is responsible for illustrating one verse of Psalm 23. Work cooperatively, and when completed, we will glue your illustrations next to each verse on the chart. You all did a lovely job of lettering the chart in markers last week, and I am sure the illustrations will be delightful.

"Snow Goose, I want you to work with these two younger students. Patrick Jr., you may work with Little Bear. Alisha, I want you and Little Ptarmigan to let Jonathan work in your group." Though he was just a baby, Jonathan wanted to sit with the other children and be involved.

After all the groups were working, Mrs. Milligan announced, "While you are drawing pictures to illustrate your verses, I am going to work with White Bear on the sounds and letters of the English alphabet. To learn to read, we all must start at the same place, no matter what our age."

White Bear and Mrs. Milligan went through the three sounds of "a": Ā as in ape, Ă as in antelope, and Ȧ as in armadillo, plus M for mule and S for sunfish, all before the groups completed their Psalm 23 pictures.

Mrs. Milligan mused, "With the progress White Bear is making on his first day, it will be only a short time before he is able to read."

CHAPTER 17

CABIN CLEANING

Andy could not remember how long he had sat on the edge of the cot, listening to the wolf howls get closer and closer to the cabin, but sometime during the night he had slumped over from sheer exhaustion and had fallen asleep.

"What a night!" Andy said to himself as he stretched. Then he started sneezing again due to the years of dust that came out of the mattress every time he moved on it.

"Well, I guess I'll start my new life here in this cabin. It's a little lighter outside, so I'm sure those wolves are asleep somewhere."

Andy went outside and gathered some firewood and small twigs for fire starter; then he came back into the cabin.

"I can at least make myself some hot water and pretend it's tea." Andy got a fire going. Then he put some fresh snow in a pot he found and hung it over the fire. When it was hot, he swished it around to clean the pot; then he poured it outdoors and got some more clean snow to melt for "tea."

"Lord, thank You for this bright fire. Thank You for this cabin and this cot. Thank You for the fireplace, the pot, and the hot water. Thank You that I am still alive. However, Lord, You know that I have no food left. This hot water is good, but it is not sustenance. You know that the only food I had all day yesterday was one can of milk and that for the past seven days, I have consumed only six cans of milk, five small flat cans of sardines, and one jar of pickled beets. I am human, and humans need food to keep them alive. Lord, I'm trusting You to supply my needs. Amen."

With that, he slowly and joyfully sipped his hot water. Still, in the back of his mind, he pondered his future with the lack of food and the wolves that he knew were out there—somewhere.

After his hot-water pretend tea, Andy set about the task of cleaning up the cabin the best he could. "For starters, I must get the dust out of this mattress." He dragged it outdoors and began to beat it against a tree. "Oh my," Andy wheezed, "I didn't realize how weak I was getting. That really tired me out." He left the mattress outdoors to soak up fresh air while he went indoors. With a rag and a pot of melted snow, he wiped layers of dirt from the windowsills. He also cleaned the two hand-hewn chairs and the old, wooden table that had once been painted bright blue. After years of neglect, most of the paint had flaked off. With a rag tied to the end of a tree branch, he mopped the wide-planked wooden floor. Next, he went outdoors and got more firewood. He added some to the fire in the fireplace and soon had it roaring once again; then he hung a fresh pot of snow over it. Finally, he sat on a chair, slumped down, and just watched the fire.

"Physical work tires me since I haven't had enough to eat. I only worked a few hours, but it feels like days! Speaking of days, I need to make myself a calendar system so I can keep track of time—that is, if I live. Now, I must not let myself think like that. But with no food, how long can I last? I must get my mind off that."

Andy went outside, and, using his hunting knife, he cut a notch in the young sapling that was growing right outside the door of the cabin. "Every day when I get up, I will cut a notch in the tree to keep track of the days."

He figured up the days since he had crashed and carved the date in the tree. "February eighth, h-m-m, three months till spring breakup. No canoes will be upriver until then."

Discouraging thoughts flooded Andy's mind again. "I wonder if I'll make it. I know I won't unless I get some food. But how will I get food when all I have is this knife? I'd have to run right up on a creature to kill it, and I just don't have enough energy left to chase any game.

"It's going to take a miracle to get me out of this predicament, but if anyone can do it, God can. He's the only One I know Who can work miracles."

Andy dragged the mattress indoors and sat on it, staring at the fire, sipping more hot water.

CHAPTER 18
TOOTHPASTE TEA

"I wonder what day this is?" Andy weakly dragged himself outside to check the notches in his sapling. "Well, I've been here three days. This makes the fourth, and I've had nothing to eat except for gnawing on some bark." He took his knife and scraped some soft pulp from the inner edge of the bark. His stomach was burning and churning from his new diet.

"Oh, my stomach feels so raw. I feel awful. I don't even want to look at another piece of bark! If only I had something to settle my stomach."

Then he thought of a remedy—toothpaste. "That's it! My toothpaste has mint in it," Andy noted, reading the ingredients on the side of the tube. He squirted some toothpaste into his hot water, stirred, and sipped.

"M-m-m, this is delicious! Good thing I bought the all-natural kind from my cousin Harry instead of the regular kind from the store. Real mint tea!"

Though the toothpaste "tea" tasted good, it was not sustenance, and Andy grew weaker and weaker as the days passed.

"Day seven at the cabin," Andy mumbled as he looked at the notches in the sapling. "I spend my nights

68

listening to wolves howl and my days sipping hot water. Now I'm even out of toothpaste!

"I am so lonely. The silence is deafening in the daytime and the wolves at night are terrifying. Lord, I'm so weak, I can barely stand up. Lord, are You listening? I've had no food for seven days. I'm so dizzy."

Then he slumped over in the snow next to his sapling and passed out.

CHAPTER 19
LONE WOLF

Andy was roused to consciousness by a warm, rough tongue licking his face. He was afraid to look, but he knew he must. Opening his eyes only a slit, he saw that he was nose to nose with a 70-kilogram (150-pound) wolf. Andy's heart began to race wildly. The wolf licked his face again. Andy squeezed his eyes tightly shut, clenched his fists, and lay perfectly still in the snow—waiting— waiting for the wolf to take a bite of him.

"I'm dead now, for sure," Andy thought. Then without uttering a word, Andy silently prayed, "Lord Jesus, Your servant is ready. I love You, and I have trusted You as my Saviour. If it be Your will, please take me quickly without allowing me to suffer too much."

Andy knew that attempting to reach for his knife was futile because he was too weak to use it effectively. So he just lay there—waiting—with his eyes closed, feeling the hot breath of the wolf on his face.

Suddenly the wolf nudged Andy's side with its nose, but Andy was still too frightened to move or open his eyes. Then the wolf nudged Andy again. Hesitantly, Andy opened his eyes and looked straight into the wolf's gray eyes. Andy glanced around. It was a lone wolf, not part of a pack. He looked again into the eyes of the wolf.

The wolf looked into Andy's eyes, not with the cold glare of a killer, but with warm eyes of compassion. The wolf leaned over and licked Andy's face again. Andy slowly extended his hand and stroked the lone wolf's ruff. Then the wolf turned and loped off into the woods.

Andy reached over to his calendar tree and pulled himself upright. He sat there stunned and dazed. Then he remembered standing dizzily by the sapling earlier. "I must have passed out from hunger," he thought. "I wonder if this is still the same day? It must be. I don't think I would be alive if I had been out here all night. The wolf pack would surely have eaten me, or I'd be frozen. It must be the same day."

Suddenly the lone wolf reappeared, but this time he had something in his mouth. He ran out of the trees directly toward Andy, who sat rigidly and held his breath.

The wolf came right up beside him and dropped a snowshoe hare and a wild ptarmigan. They were freshly killed and still warm and limp. Andy stared at the dead hare and ptarmigan. Then he stared at the wolf. The wolf pushed the dead hare with his nose until it rolled over beside Andy.

"So, I guess this is a gift, huh, ol' boy? Well, if you knew how hungry I am, I guess you'd know how grateful I am."

Andy slowly reached into his sheath and drew out his knife, keeping both eyes on the wolf. He still was not quite sure of the wolf's intentions. Unbelievably, the wolf sat down on his haunches and stared back at Andy.

Beginning to feel almost comfortable in the wolf's presence, Andy began to clean the hare with his hunting knife. "You know, I've never eaten raw meat before," said Andy still staring at the wolf, "but I know I need the food and I simply have no energy with which to build a fire. Would you like to dine with me, wolf?" Andy queried as he took a bite of the warm flesh of the hare.

Taking cue from Andy, the wolf also began to eat his meal—wild ptarmigan, feathers and all.

Andy had only eaten a few bites of the hindquarter when he started to feel full. He stopped eating, knowing that, if he ate too much on a seven-day empty stomach, he would vomit it back up. He saved the other hindquarter, both front quarters, and the back, but he reached out to the wolf with the head and entrails as an offering of thanks.

The wolf gladly accepted. When he finished eating, he lay down contentedly by Andy's feet.

Andy was still sitting in the snow by his sapling. "You know, wolf, I'm going to name you 'Lone Wolf' because you are not with a pack. You're all right," he said gently, stroking the wolf. "People could learn a good lesson from you, Lone Wolf. Sometimes when we run with the pack, we are mean and ruthless, but if we stand alone, we can allow goodness and a caring spirit to shine forth."

Barely twenty minutes after eating the piece of hare, Andy could feel strength coming back into his body. "Dear God, forgive me. Just when I thought You weren't listening, You sent this wolf along to feed me. Just as You sent the ravens to feed Elijah when he was hiding by the brook Cherith, so today You have sent this wolf to feed me beside the Mackenzie River. Thank You, Lord. Thank You ever so much for taking care of me!"

Back in Amaroqvik God was blessing also. White Bear rose to his feet during a church service and read Psalm 23 from his Bible. Then he proudly announced, "Since I have been attending the mission school, I can sing the songs from the hymnal all by myself. I feel like the whole world has opened up for me now that I can read. I know I have a lot more to learn, but I am so very happy. Even at my age, I am learning to read, and I am grateful to Mrs. Milligan and all the students and my wife for helping me and encouraging me."

With that he sat down, and the whole congregation rejoiced with him.

CHAPTER 20
SPRING AT LAST

One May morning, Alisha, Snow Goose, and Little Ptarmigan came bounding into the Milligan kitchen, wet snow flying off their parkas and boots. "It's spring! It's spring!" exclaimed Little Ptarmigan with all the enthusiasm of an eight-year-old.

"How do you know?" queried Mrs. Milligan with a knowing smile.

"Because we found crocuses coming up through the snow!"

"And we brought you some, Mrs. Milligan," continued her sister, Snow Goose, as she held out a mittened hand that clasped a bouquet of delicate white and yellow flowers.

Alisha leaned over and kissed her mother on the cheek. "See, Mom, all the children at school love you. You don't have just three children—you have lots!"

"You all are too much," chuckled Mrs. Milligan as she reached out and they all hugged in a football-type huddle. "I love all of you too, and the crocuses are beautiful. Let me get a jar of water for them."

"See, I told you it was spring," Little Ptarmigan went on. "Now maybe somebody will find Andy and his plane."

A somber silence fell over the room. Nobody had even mentioned Andy's name in the past month. For the first few weeks that he was missing, folks had faithfully prayed for him almost every service. But as time passed, they all felt that the inevitable had occurred—Andy had either died on impact or later of injuries; the wolves had devoured him; or, worse yet, he had suffered a long, slow death from starvation and exposure to the weather.

To break the sad stillness, Mrs. Milligan interjected, "It is possible that when spring breakup occurs, he will be able to get through." But in her heart she felt certain that Andy was already dead.

Downtown at the general trading store, most of the townspeople were discussing the weather in tones of exuberance and exultation. "Yes, Sam, I know you're out of flour and cornmeal here at the store, but it won't be long now," said White Bear to the storekeeper.

"I heard the river bubbling under the ice on my way over here today," added Pastor Milligan as he walked through the door of Sam's General Store. "Say, do you have any salt left, Sam? My wife has two jars of cabbage that she canned last year and put in back of the linen closet. She forgot all about them until she pulled out our good tablecloth, and there they were! They're about as flat as can be. We need to spice them up a bit."

"I have no salt left, but I do have half a scoop of peppercorns here," Sam said. "She could boil down some caribou, cabbage, and peppercorns and make quite a nice soup. You do have some caribou left, don't you?"

"Yes, we are still thanking the Lord for that meat. It would have been disastrous for this village if White Bear's search party had not shared the caribou."

"Speaking of search parties," interjected White Bear, "do you think Andy will turn up after the spring breakup?"

"In all honesty, White Bear, I believe he has gone to be with the Lord. We did all we could, and a real air search was impossible with the weather conditions that have prevailed during the past two and a half months. I think we have to face reality."

"Well, Pastor," White Bear continued, "I have learned that with God, nothing is impossible, and I'm just going to keep praying and trusting."

"I agree," Sam called out. "I've been in these parts for forty-six years. Came here as a boy with my daddy, who was a trapper, and I've seen stranger things in my time. Well, back in the winter of '67, there was snow piled up 6 meters (20 feet) deep. Buried all the cabins. We went for weeks without eatin' anything except spruce bark tea, and I'm still here to tell the story. Besides, this is spring. It's the time of new life and miracles."

"Speaking of miracles," said Pastor Milligan, "my wife wants some calico cloth to make a new dress for the end-of-school awards banquet."

"Well, she may get her wish," Sam chortled. "Just got word today on my radio that the freighter is due in three weeks because of the early spring breakup."

"All right!" White Bear exclaimed. "You get Patrick Jr. and I'll get Little Bear. We'll all drive up to Tuktoyaktuk in your jeep to meet the freighter and buy our year's supplies."

"Of course, but we mustn't forget the ladies in our lives, White Bear. We'll have to go home and tell our wives and daughters so they can spend the next three weeks making their shopping lists!"

CHAPTER 21

FISHING TRIP DISCOVERY

Day by day Andy's spirit soared, and his strength was renewed by Lone Wolf's frequent deposits of "groceries." One day it would be two ptarmigans; another day a snowshoe hare; or, most often, a mouthful of voles. Lone Wolf always brought his kill and laid it at Andy's feet and then waited for Andy to dole it out as he pleased. Lone Wolf was always duly rewarded. Then one day the big lot came—an elderly elk who had succumbed to the elements and lack of food himself. He was very tough and bony, but he was sustenance for Andy and Lone Wolf for four weeks.

As spring approached, the two spent most of their time outdoors, enjoying the lengthening hours of spring sunlight glistening on the snow. At night, Andy went inside and lit a roaring fire, but Lone Wolf insisted on staying outdoors. Andy had thrown an old tarpaulin on the ground between the stoop and the calendar tree, and that's where Lone Wolf spent his nights.

Each night when the wolf pack started to howl, Lone Wolf answered them. Instead of the howls coming closer and closer to the cabin like they used to, now the howls receded farther and farther into the woods with each reply from Lone Wolf.

One day Andy spoke to his new companion. "Okay, ol' boy, let's go fishing today. What do you say, Lone Wolf?"

Lone Wolf replied by panting and running circles around Andy's legs.

"I think that's an affirmative. I've been hearing the river boil and churn for about three weeks now, so there should be some fish coming up from the bottom. Let's go!"

Andy and Lone Wolf set out across the clearing with some ancient, rusty fishing gear from the cabin and some fresh entrails from Lone Wolf's latest "grocery shopping."

"Well, if these vole 'innards' don't attract fish, I don't know what will," continued Andy as they slopped through the thick, melting snow that was the consistency of a chocolate shake.

"Snow covered with a thick crust of ice is easy to travel on, but this thick slush makes for slow traveling," puffed Andy.

When they arrived at a place along the river that Andy deemed a good fishing spot, he sat on a big, round rock and began to untangle the fishing line. Lone Wolf flopped down nearby atop a large, flat rock that formed a ledge over the edge of the river.

"Sunning yourself, I see," Andy called to him. "I guess that's fair. You've been finding all the food for both of us for several weeks now, so I guess it's my turn. You just relax. We'll have salmon for supper tonight."

Just then, Andy heard strange noises from downriver. Because of the way sound carried in this vast country, it was probably still a few kilometers (miles) away, whatever it was. But the noise broke the silence and somewhat disturbed Andy. Lone Wolf heard it too, and sitting up on his haunches, he put his nose in the air and started sniffing short, rapid whiffs of air. Slowly he lay back down, but continued to make low, almost inaudible growls.

Andy decided to let nothing stand in the way of his spring fishing event and continued working on the line. After a bit, the line was straightened. He rubbed some fat from a hare onto the handle of the reel and was in business. He had been rubbing fat on that old reel nightly for about two weeks, and it had loosened up nicely despite its ugly, rusty appearance.

"It won't take long now, ol' boy," Andy called over his shoulder as he made a nice cast into the river. He reeled in his line and cast again. His line tugged. He tugged back and jerked up a beautiful salmon. "Look, Lone Wolf! Lunch!"

He cast again and reeled in again, three more times and three more fish. Just as he was slapping the fourth fish on the rock, he distinctly heard human voices. Lone Wolf heard them too and began growling in earnest.

About 400 meters (one-quarter of a mile) downriver, Andy saw two men in a canoe, one old and grizzled, and the other younger and heavier with brown bushy hair and a full reddish-brown beard.

"Trappers! What do you know! We've been discovered!"

Lone Wolf leaped from his ledge onto the round rock where Andy stood. He fairly wrapped his long, lean body around Andy's legs. His big head and ruff peered out from Andy's side. Both Andy and Lone Wolf stood frozen with anticipation—Andy's from joy and Lone Wolf's from anxiety.

As the canoe approached, Andy called a greeting. "Hi! I'm Andrew Johnson, pilot. Some folks call me Aviator Andy. Stop for a while and I'll fix you lunch."

Lone Wolf continued to emit low growls, and both men stayed in the canoe, eyeing him. "Lone Wolf, it's okay. All humans aren't bad.

"Gentlemen, if you have a bite of food to offer the wolf here, I think he'll understand you mean no harm."

Neither man had spoken yet, but the grizzled one reached out over the edge of the canoe with a piece of caribou jerky. He barely held the end of it with his

fingertips while Lone Wolf, keeping his distance, reached his head out and with his foreteeth grasped the opposite end of the 15-centimeter (6-inch) strip of jerky. Wolf and man eyed one another cautiously, but less suspiciously now.

The younger, bushy-haired man laughed at the whole scene and said, "I'm Burt Redgrave. Most folks just call me Red. Here, animal, have a biscuit," he called as he threw a pork cracklin' biscuit in the general direction of Lone Wolf. Lone Wolf accepted it heartily.

The thin, grizzled man took one paddle and pushed the wide, red aluminum canoe closer to the rocky shore. As he stepped out, he gruffly said to Andy, "So what brings you here in the middle of nowhere, lad?"

Andy commenced telling him the story of his earlier intended flight to Amaroqvik on which he was carrying food and medicine to a missionary family. He told of the wind shear, the ensuing crash, his trek here to the cabin, and the appearance of Lone Wolf.

"So you're a religious fella, huh?"

"Well, I don't particularly relate to the word 'religious,' sir," Andy replied, "but I do believe in God. I have trusted Jesus Christ as my Saviour, and He has forgiven my sins. I believe the best way I can serve Him is by helping His people. That's why I fly supplies to missionaries.

"Why don't you gentlemen come on up to the cabin, and I'll fry up this fresh fish for all of us? Your legs must be stiff and sore from sitting in that canoe for so long. Where did you come from today, anyway? There's no town for at least 200 kilometers (125 miles)."

The old man, who still had not even introduced himself, spoke up, "We set out five days ago from Norman Wells. Been settin' up camp every night along the way. We wanted to check our traps one last time for this season. And yes, we'd be much obliged to eat lunch with you. I'm Slim Peterson."

"Welcome. Come on; follow me."

The three men trudged through the slush while Lone Wolf loped ahead toward the cabin in anticipation of a fish dinner. They all ate heartily of fish fried in hare fat, and Lone Wolf enjoyed the heads, fins, tails, and entrails.

It was decided that the trappers would spend the night at the cabin; then early the next morning, Red would canoe Andy the week-or-so journey to Amaroqvik. Slim would use the cabin as his trapping base until Red's return. Lone Wolf seemed a bit uneasy and even came indoors that night to sleep under Andy's cot. The other two men threw sleeping bags on the floor.

"Coffee!" Andy exclaimed the next morning as he threw his legs over the side of the cot. "I smell coffee!

Do you know how long it's been since I've had anything to drink except hot water, toothpaste 'tea,' or spruce bark tea? That smells great!"

Red replied, "Well, first one up makes the coffee, and today that was me. Do you have anything you want to load in the canoe? We'll want to get an early start and make as many kilometers (miles) as we can today."

"Only this wolf and my backpack," replied Andy, reaching down to rub Lone Wolf's ruff.

"The wolf?" queried Red.

"Oh, I know I can't take him. I'll be getting another plane and be in the air most of the time. That's no life for a wolf, but I'll miss him intensely. God used him to save my life. Without him, I would have starved to death weeks ago," Andy recounted as a mist covered his eyes. "God and Lone Wolf were the only ones I had to talk to all winter." Andy pulled Lone Wolf's head over to his leg and continued to rub his ruff.

"Oh, quit moanin' over that animal. I'll keep him company," Slim retorted as he tossed a pork cracklin' biscuit over to Lone Wolf.

Never one to refuse food, Lone Wolf gobbled the biscuit in one bite; then rising to his feet, he edged his way over to the rough chair where Slim sat.

"I reckon you'd be a mighty fine huntin' partner," Slim said as he offered Lone Wolf a second biscuit.

"Besides, I'll need someone to talk with until Red gets back."

Lone Wolf seemed to understand the transfer of partnership, and he lay down by Slim's feet in front of the fireplace.

"So you're going soft on me now, huh, Lone Wolf?" teased Andy. "Are you going to become a house dog and lie in front of the fireplace? You certainly deserve it. Enjoy."

When they had finished eating biscuits and drinking coffee, Andy walked over to the fireplace and stroked Lone Wolf's back one last time; then he strapped on his knife, picked up his backpack, and headed out the door with Red. He stopped at the calendar tree. He counted ninety-one notches—only three months, but it felt like eternity.

CHAPTER 22

JOY COMETH IN THE MORNING

"Dad! Mom! Everybody! Guess who's at Sam's General Store!" Patrick Jr. excitedly called out as he flew through the kitchen door, mud flying off his boots and splattering onto the wall.

"I don't know," replied his mother sternly, "but he had better be important, considering the mess you're making."

Patrick Jr. rushed right on. "It's Andy! Andy, the missionary pilot! He's up at the store right now!"

"How do you know this, son?" queried Pastor Milligan.

"Because I was just there, Dad."

"Maybe it was someone who looked like him, dear," added his mother.

"No, no! You don't understand. I was just talking to him. A trapper just brought him to Amaroqvik. He's up there right now telling everybody all about the crash and his pet wolf and how he lived on toothpaste 'tea.' Come on!"

"Okay! What are we waiting for?" replied Pastor Milligan.

"Praise God! Andy's still alive and well," chimed in Mrs. Milligan as she donned her sweater and scarf.

Eagerly, all three marched through the mud to Sam's General Store.

"Andy! I never thought I'd see you again on this earth," exclaimed Pastor Milligan as he embraced Andy.

"For awhile there, I never thought I'd see another human being, either. I'm still thanking the Lord for sending Red and Slim upriver. Pastor Milligan, meet Burt Redgrave, Red for short."

Pastor Milligan reached out and shook Red's hand. "We sure are grateful to you for bringing our friend back to civilization."

"Think nothin' of it, sir," Red replied. "It was the only decent human thing to do, seein' how he was stuck out there all alone for so long."

"Where are you two staying?" asked Mrs. Milligan, clasping Andy's hand and looking intently into his big blue eyes. "You know you are like a son to us, Andy. You are so dear to our hearts."

"Well, ma'am, you're all like family to me too, especially since my mom died when I was only thirteen." He placed his strong hand on top of hers. "I don't know where we'll stay. We just arrived about half an hour ago, and I hadn't thought about needing a place to stay."

"It's settled, then," interjected Pastor Milligan. "You'll both come to our house and stay as long as you need. You can share Patrick's room, and we'll put Jonathan in with us."

"Tomorrow is Wednesday night church service. We'll have a big carry-in supper at the church for you," said Mrs. Milligan excitedly. "Son, go spread the word."

The supply freighter had arrived two days earlier so there was plenty of everything. Sea Gull brought a huge tray of fresh, fried fish and a basket full of juicy berries. Snow Goose, Little Ptarmigan, and Alisha got together and made a big batch of cornmeal cookies. Everybody brought something to share, and there was much rejoicing.

Even as it states in Psalm 30, ". . . joy cometh in the morning," and in Psalm 126, "They that sow in tears shall reap in joy." For the congregation at Amaroqvik, just as in the days of Queen Esther, this was ". . . the month which was turned unto them from sorrow to joy, and from mourning into a good day: that they should make them days of feasting and joy . . ." (Esther 9:22).